Happy as a Dog's Tail

HAPPY AS A

DOG'S TAIL

by
ANNA SWIR

Translated by Czeslaw Milosz with Leonard Nathan
Introduction by Czeslaw Milosz
Afterword by Czeslaw Milosz and Leonard Nathan

HARCOURT BRACE JOVANOVICH, PUBLISHERS
San Diego   New York   London

Library of Congress Cataloging in Publication Data
Świrszczyńska, Anna.
    Happy as a dog's tail.
    I. Miłosz, Czesław. II. Nathan, Leonard, 1924–
III. Title.
PG7178.W57A25 1985   891.8'517   85-8675
ISBN 0-15-138465-7

Photograph of Anna Swir by Neider-Foryś
Designed by Kate Nichols
Printed in the United States of America

First edition

A B C D E

Contents

v

Stanza breaks between pages are indicated by a _____.

Introduction

Question: What is the central theme of these poems?
Answer: Flesh. Flesh in love ecstasy, flesh in pain, flesh
in terror, flesh afraid of loneliness, exuberant, running,
lazy, flesh of a woman giving birth, resting, snoring, doing
her morning calisthenics, feeling the flow of time or reducing time to one instant. By such a clear delineation
of her subject matter, Anna Swir achieves in her sensual
and, one could say, fierce poetry a nearly calligraphic
neatness.

I have wondered why the poems of Anna Swir's that
I have read aloud in translation were so liked by American
audiences. Among the many women poets in America
there are several who write about a woman's body with
a directness similar to hers, and yet the listeners distin-
guished in her a new tone, of rare intensity. The differ-
ence is, I believe, that she is more objective than her
American contemporaries, because the body, including
her own, is for her both the subject of perceptions and
an object observed with detachment. "If people find her
poems appealing, why don't you translate more and make
a book?" asked a friend of mine. His suggestion, however,
would not have been enough to prompt me, if not for a

special dimension I discover in these poems' very earthiness.

During our century various kinds of language traditionally used to cope with our anxiety in the face of existence have been stricken by sudden obsolescence. The language of theology lost its hold over the minds of even the most fervent believers. The language of philosophy became technical to mask the avowal that philosophy is hardly possible. The language of science in its optimistic nineteenth-century variety has suffered a loss of self-assurance. In this situation a poet trying to come to terms with experience has had to discover his or her own improvised means. That was not the case in the past, when poets worked with constant reference to images provided by religion and religiously oriented philosophy. Perhaps now poets are returning to the time of the pre-Socratics, to the unity of poetry and philosophy not yet conscious of their separate claims. In the poetry of the last decades there is a groping in that direction, a persistent effort to start from scratch in attempting to define our human condition.

In Anna Swir's vision, we are alone in a world without gods, exposed every moment to total annihilation, helpless in the face of terminal illness and old age, driven to seek in each other's arms physical love as the only possible source of warmth and peace. Yet the exploration of the only tangible thing which is given us as ourself, namely our body, leads her to a paradoxical duality. Her personae are trapped by their flesh but also distinct from it, for they are consciousness, ever present, perhaps with rare exceptions—flashes of purely physical bliss. Her poetry is about not being identical with one's body, about sharing its joys and pains and still rebelling against its laws. By a curious reversal, proceeding from a radically somatic approach she revives the centuries-old philosophical meditation on our dual nature always tending to transcend its limits—what was once called a dialogue between the body and the soul. Yet our place in the world, as we construct it in our imagination, changed as the division into clearly delineated material and spiritual realms disappeared. The basic feeling of amazement at our conscious existence on the brink of vanishing, a feeling always alive in any thinking person, calls today for a new expression, as traditional ways of expressing it do not mean much to us anymore. Reading Anna Swir's poems, we are confronted with this amazement in its nakedness; perhaps, given her central preoccupation, she deserves to be called a metaphysical poet.

Anna Swir (Świrszczyńska) was born in Warsaw in 1909, the daughter of a painter. As she says herself, she literally grew up in her father's workshop, sleeping and preparing her lessons there. The poverty in which the family lived forced her early to look for work. In her own words: "I was then terribly shy, ugly, and crushed by a mountain of complexes." She put herself through the university, studying medieval and baroque Polish literature, discovering the Polish language of the fifteenth century, which according to her is the most vigorous. Her first poems, published in the 1930s, bear the marks both of her upbringing in the artistic milieu (images taken from paintings and albums of reproductions) and of her fascination with the Middle Ages. These are mostly short poems in prose, sophisticated miniatures, from which any personal accents are carefully eliminated. The form of the miniature was to return later, while the reticence about her personal life was to disappear.

The experience of war radically changed Anna. She shared the fate of Warsaw, beginning with the siege by the Nazis in September 1939, continuing through the years of the occupation, and ending with the final destruction of the city in the fall of 1944. A member of the Resistance, she wrote for underground publications. During the sixty-three days of the Warsaw Uprising in August–September 1944, she was a military nurse in an improvised hospital. A survivor—once she waited for an hour expecting to be executed—she says: "War made me another person. Only then did my own life and the life of my contemporaries enter my poems." However, as she confesses, she had great difficulty finding a proper form for what she had seen and lived through. Thirty years had to elapse before she succeeded in writing a volume of short poem-pictures on the Warsaw Uprising, *Building the Barricade* (1974). The technique of the miniature she elaborated in her youth now served a different purpose.

No less slow was her maturing as the poet of the present volume, primarily a poet of personal life, of love and love's pain. For several years she was known mostly as the author of poems and stories for children. Her volumes of poetry *Wind* and *I Am a Woman*, straightforward in their sensuality, were published when she was over sixty, in 1970 and 1972, respectively. *I Am a Woman* has a strong feminist bent, defending, for example, the right of elderly women to sex. Then came *Happy as a Dog's Tail* (1978), from which I borrow the title of this book, in accordance with the wishes of the author. (The title perhaps raises the question: does the dog wag the tail, or the tail the dog?)

Anna is not an abstract figure for me. We made our literary debut more or less at the same time before the war, and later I used to see her, though not often, in underground Warsaw, where writers would attend clandestine meetings. When, after many years, I met her in Poland in summer 1981, she seemed to me much stronger—in the physical sense, too—than she had been in her youth: an attractive woman, lithe, with a ruddy complexion, her hair like the white mane of a fairy-tale witch. I told her that I always valued her poetry, though at that moment I did not expect I would prepare a volume of it in English.

Somehow the decision matured slowly and became a reality three years later, in 1984. Then, but not before the volume had been completed, I told her about my endeavors in a letter. From her answer I could see that the news made her genuinely happy. I did not realize that she was at the time dangerously ill. A few weeks later I was stunned to hear she had died of cancer. Perhaps we all strongly believe in certain modes of behavior which should be effective means against death: an ecstatic approval of life, a clear awareness of our precarious human condition. To me Anna Swir seemed immune simply because it was difficult to imagine a person writing her type of poetry who was not strongly alive. What remained now was to think with relief that at least I brought some joy to the last days of her earthly peregrination.

That she did not write literary criticism is to her credit. Yet she was an artist well aware of what she was doing. In one of her infrequent pronouncements I find the following remarks on poetry:

"By expressing reality, it masters and overcomes it, it creates around man a delicate, tender miniworld to protect him from the dreadfulness of the maxiworld. Every Negro or Eskimo lullaby is a warm nest for a human nestling, enveloping its helplessness. Let our words be as necessary and useful as once were words of magic. This is an unachievable ideal."

"The poet should be as sensitive as an aching tooth."

"[The poet] has a conscience with room to grow; what does not as yet shock and outrage others shocks and outrages him."

"How to write poems? There will be as many answers as people who write. Personally, I consider that nothing can replace the psychosomatic phenomenon of inspiration. This seems to me the only biologically natural way for a poem to be born and gives the poem something like a biological right to exist. A poet becomes then an antenna capturing the voices of the world, a medium expressing his own subconscious and the collective subconscious. For one moment he possesses wealth usually inaccessible to him, and he loses it when that moment is over."

"The goal of words in poetry is to grow up to the contents, yet that goal cannot ever be attained, for only a small part of psychic energy which dwells in a poet incarnates itself in words. In fact, every poem has the right to ask for a new poetics created only once to express the contents, also given only once, of a poem. Style is the enemy of a poet, and its greatest merit would be its nonexistence. We could say in paradoxical abbreviation that a writer has two tasks. The first—to create one's own style. The second—to destroy one's own style. The second is more difficult and takes more time."

Hers were quite severe demands and, I am sure, not to everybody's liking. Contrary to the widespread view that poetry is an act of spinning a linguistic thread, she advanced the idea of a transparent style aspiring to nonexistence because it strives to seize what she termed "contents." In this she proved loyal to her own development as a poet: from the highly stylized, detached miniatures of her youth to a form which is artless in appearance and, so to say, confesses that it is inadequate for the overbearing passions of a being all flesh and blood.

The poems in this book appear in the order of the published volumes of Anna Swir, with the exception of the poems from *Building the Barricade* quoted in the Afterword. That volume also exists in a bilingual edition, with translations by Magnus J. Krynski and Robert A. Maguire (Kraków: Wydawnictwo Literackie, 1979).

After I completed the translations of the poems, I showed them to my friend Leonard Nathan, whose poetic insight I trust. He read them carefully and marked all the places where the wording seemed to him doubtful, from the point of view of either American idiom or meaning. Then we sat down over the script and worked together on the marked passages. As I value his contribution, I feel he should be considered a cotranslator.

WIND

I AM FILLED WITH LOVE

I am filled with love
as a great tree with the wind,
as a sponge with the ocean,
as a great life with suffering,
as time with death.

HAPPINESS

My hair is happy
and my skin is happy.
My skin quivers with happiness.

I breathe happiness instead of air,
slowly and deeply
as a man who avoided a mortal danger.

Tears roll down my face,
I do not know it.
I forget I still have a face.
My skin is singing,
I shiver.

I feel time's duration
as it is felt in the hour of death.
As if my sense of time alone were grasping the world,
as if existence were time only.
Immersed in terrifying
magnificence
I feel every second of happiness, as it arrives,
fills up, bursts into flower
according to its own natural way,
unhurried as a fruit,
astounding as a deity.

Now
I begin to scream.
I am screaming. I leave my body.
I do not know whether I am human anymore

how could anyone know that, screaming with happiness.
Yet one dies from such screaming,
thus I am dying from happiness.
On my face there are probably no more tears,
my skin probably does not sing by now.
I don't know whether I still have a skin,
from me to my skin
is too far to know.

Soon I will go.
I do not shiver any longer,
I do not breathe any longer.
I don't know whether I still have
something to breathe with.

I feel time's duration,
how perfectly I feel time's duration.

I sink
I sink into time.

WOMAN UNBORN

I am not born as yet,
five minutes before my birth.
I can still go back
into my unbirth.
Now it's ten minutes before,
now, it's one hour before birth.
I go back,
I run
into my minus life.

I walk through my unbirth as in a tunnel
with bizarre perspectives.
Ten years before,
a hundred and fifty years before,
I walk, my steps thump,
a fantastic journey through epochs
in which there was no me.

How long is my minus life,
nonexistence so much resembles immortality.

Here is Romanticism, where I could have been a spinster,
Here is the Renaissance, where I would have been
an ugly and unloved wife of an evil husband,
The Middle Ages, where I would have carried water in a tavern.

I walk still further,
what an echo,
my steps thump

through my minus life,
through the reverse of life.
I reach Adam and Eve,
nothing is seen anymore, it's dark.
Now my nonexistence dies already
with the trite death of mathematical fiction.
As trite as the death of my existence would have been
had I been really born.

TROUBLES WITH THE SOUL AT MORNING CALISTHENICS

Lying down I lift my legs,
my soul by mistake jumps into my legs.
This is not convenient for her,
besides, she must branch,
for the legs are two.

When I stand on my head
my soul sinks down to my head.
She is then in her place.

But how long can you stand on your head,
especially if you do not know
how to stand on your head.

MYSELF AND MY PERSON

There are moments
when I feel more clearly than ever
that I am in the company
of my own person.
This comforts and reassures me,
this heartens me,
just as my tridimensional body
is heartened by my own authentic shadow.

There are moments
when I really feel more clearly than ever
that I am in the company
of my own person.

I stop
at a street corner to turn left
and I wonder what would happen
if my own person walked to the right.

Until now that has not happened
but it does not settle the question.

MOVEMENT

I will leave space,
I will enter space.
I will leave time,
I will enter time.
I will leave a cause,
I will enter a cause.

Leaving, entering
I will not notice
that by then I am no more.

MATERNITY

I gave birth to life.
It went out of my entrails
and asks for the sacrifice of my life
as does an Aztec deity.
I lean over a little puppet,
we look at each other
with four eyes.

"You are not going to defeat me," I say.
"I won't be an egg which you would crack
in a hurry for the world,
a footbridge that you would take on the way to your life.
I will defend myself."

I lean over a little puppet,
I notice
a tiny movement of a tiny finger
which a little while ago was still in me,
in which, under a thin skin,
my own blood flows.
And suddenly I am flooded
by a high, luminous wave
of humility.
Powerless, I drown.

Do I thus adore myself
in the fruit of my flesh,
do I offer myself for a sacrifice

to a cannibal god of instinct?
Where will I get the strength to resist
what is so weak?

Necessary for the little puppet as air,
I let myself unresisting be swallowed by love
as the air lets itself be swallowed
by these tiny life-starved lungs.

THE LAST MAN IS DYING

Night
submerges me.
In the whole world there is nothing alive,
this is the end of the world.

I say to that night
which wants to enter me by the throat
as the sea enters a sinking ship:
"I am the last man,
don't swallow me."
"I must swallow you,
the last man."
"Then first extinguish the light in my head."
"It will shine till the end."
"Then let something alive visit me once more,
a rat, a louse, or a snake."
"They won't come, neither a louse nor a snake,
there is nothing alive anymore."

Darkness dark as the inside of an immense brain,
my eyes utterly open,
what are eyes for.
Night enters me by the throat
as the sea into a sinking ship.
Hot entrails
cool very slowly.
Night grasps the convex heart
of the last man with its fingers.
It closes on itself
very slowly.

A VISIT

In a home for incurables
I visited a woman who was about to die.
She embraced me,
I felt through her gray shirt
the tiny bones of her brittle body
which would no longer arouse lust or tenderness.

"I don't want this, take me away."
Near us, a retarded woman was vomiting.

SEVENTY YEARS

He never wanted to enter my place.
"I stink, Mrs. S., it's my feet.
They're rotting,
every day I spread ashes on them,
ash has a mystical meaning,
I brought you some apples from my garden."

Once he wrote me a letter, that he would poison himself
with rat poison.
I arrived too late,
his wife was crying.
"He studied yogas, Mrs. S.
A retired stationmaster.
He collected old cans, newspapers, bolts,
his room full, read mystics.
At night he would stand in the garden
in his drawers.
Hands raised,
he waited for the revelation of the truth
for seventy years.
Longer obviously he could not."

Their women neighbors said to me:
"It's fortunate for her that he died.
She had to spread ashes every day on them.
Pus, you understand,
It stank bad, he hollered at her."

TEARS

The old woman cries,
she coddles herself in her crying
as a bird in its nest.
She sinks
into the depth of crying.
She immerses herself
in dark immersion.
Tears run down her face
like little warm animals.
They stroke her old face,
they take pity on her.

The last rapture
of tears.

TERMINALLY ILL

Every morning he is astounded again,
always for the first time,
every time more violently than before.

He is astounded relentlessly,
with impressive energy,
passionately, fiercely, vehemently,
till he is out of breath.

He pants with astonishment,
he chokes,
he gluts himself on astonishment,
he drowns like a puppy thrown into deep water,
he shivers, trembles, cries with astonishment.

That the affliction came to him
against which there is no help.

MY SUFFERING

My suffering
is useful to me.

It gives me the privilege
to write on the suffering of others.

My suffering is a pencil
with which I write.

LONELINESS

Loneliness,
the pearl of loneliness growing immense,
I took refuge in it.
A space
which expands,
in it I grow immense.
Silence, the source of voices.
Immobility, the mother of motion.

I am alone.
I am alone and so I am nothing.
What a happiness.
I am nothing, so I can be everything.
Existence without essence,
essence without existence, freedom.

I am pure as a thing that is not,
secure as the Platonic idea,
rich as a possibility.
Laughing I stretch my hands
to a thousand of my splendid futures.
I may become foam on the sea
and attain its joy of transience.
Or a jellyfish and possess for good
the whole prettiness of a jellyfish.
Or a bird with its joy of flight,
or a stone with its joy of eternity,
or the Milky Way.

———

I am alone, I am strong.
Loneliness protects me.
I am alone, and so I am not,
I am not, and so I exist
perfectly, as does perfection,
diversely, as does diversity.

Later, people will come. They will give me
a skin, color for my eyes, sex and a name.
They will give me the past and the future
of the species.

SONG OF PLENITUDE

Plenitude, oh what a plenitude,
Strength, oh what a strength.
I am full as if I were a pregnant star,
I am strong as if I could exist
all alone in space.

Out of suffering joy arose,
I have suffered, therefore I have the right
to exist so strongly.
I have gone through hell, therefore today I enter
the heaven of serenity,
a round heaven of a strong serenity,
of a serenity growing in power,
of a power growing in power,
as if into the voice of a pipe organ,
as if into an expanding inundation of light.
I enter into a lasting light.

That light is singing,
I am singing.
I am one of a million voices,
one of a million rays,
I am shining. The situation
is indecently mystical,
I can't help it, I say how it is.

Light flows from my body,
from my head, from my twin breasts.
From the ten fingers of my hands,

from the ten toes of my feet,
light flows.
I am spilled around,
I am spun out, I am spread about,
My skin disappears,
I fuse with things that are not me,
I dissolve in everything.
Once dissolved in anything
I don't exist,
that is, I exist in a way indescribably powerful.

This is death and immortality,
this is, maybe, Nirvana.
I apologize for that word but really this is it.

TO BE A WOMAN

A WOMAN TALKS TO HER THIGH

It is only thanks to your good looks
I can take part
in the rites of love

Mystical ecstasies,
treasons delightful
as a crimson lipstick,
a perverse rococo
of psychological involutions,
sweetness of carnal longings
that take your breath,
pits of despair
sinking to the very bottom of the world:
all this I owe to you.

How tenderly every day I should
lash you with a whip of cold water,
if you alone allow me to possess
beauty and wisdom
irreplaceable.

The souls of my lovers
open to me in a moment of love
and I have them in my dominion.

I look as does a sculptor
on his work
at their faces snapped shut with eyelids,
martyred by ecstasy,

made dense
by happiness.
I read as does an angel
thoughts in their skulls,
I feel in my hand
a beating human heart,
I listen to the words
which are whispered by one human to another
in the frankest moment of one's life.

I enter their souls,
I wander
by a road of delight or of horror
to lands as inconceivable
as the bottoms of the oceans.
Later on, heavy with treasures
I come slowly
to myself.

O, many riches,
many precious truths
growing immense in a metaphysical echo,
many initiations
delicate and startling
I owe to you, my thigh.

The most exquisite refinement of my soul
would not give me any of those treasures
if not for the clear, smooth charm
of an amoral little animal.

SHE DOES NOT REMEMBER

She was an evil stepmother.
In her old age she is slowly dying
in an empty hovel.

She shudders
like a clutch of burnt paper.
She does not remember that she was evil.
But she knows
that she feels cold.

THE OLD WOMAN

Her beauty
is like Atlantis.
It is yet to be discovered.
Thousands of humorists
have written on her erotic desires.
The most gifted of them
entered the school reading lists.
Only her making love with the devil
had the seriousness
of fire around the stake
and was within the human imagination just as was that fire.

Mankind created for her
the most abusive
words of the world.

THE GREATEST LOVE

She is sixty. She lives
the greatest love of her life.

She walks arm-in-arm with her dear one,
her hair streams in the wind.
Her dear one says:
"You have hair like pearls."

Her children say:
"Old fool."

THREE BODIES

A pregnant woman
lies at night by her man.
In her belly
a child moved.
"Put your hand on my belly,"
says the woman.
"What moved so lightly
is a tiny hand or leg
of our child.
It will be mine and yours
though only I have to bear it."

The man nestles close to her,
they both feel the same.
In the woman a child moves.

And the three bodies
pool their warmth
at night, when a pregnant woman
lies by her man.

YOU ARE WARM

You are warm
like a big dog. I bask
in your warmth. I immerse myself
in purity.

Every day I put on my neck
the corals of your young enchantment.
I plait into my hair your tenderness.
Your calm
strokes me on the head.

You have the virgin charm
of a being who has never experienced
the kiss of pain or the embrace of fear.

Leaning over
I look into your eyes.
Undisturbed by thought, they reflect
the sky.

I SLEEP IN BLUE PAJAMAS

I sleep in blue pajamas,
at my right my child sleeps.
I have never cried,
I will never die.

I sleep in blue pajamas,
at my left my man sleeps.
I have never knocked my head against the wall,
I have never screamed out of fear.

How large this bed is
if it has room enough
for such happiness.

WHAT IS A PINEAL GLAND

You lie asleep,
warm as a small heating plant.
Your lungs move, viscera digest,
glands diligently work,
biological processes of your sleep
make grow
the vegetation of dreams.

Do you belong to me?
I myself do not belong to myself.

I touch my skin,
lungs move inside me,
viscera digest,
the body performs its work
with which I am not well acquainted.
I know so little about the activity of the pineal gland.
Really, what do I have in common
with my body.

I touch your skin and my skin,
I am not in you
and you are not in me..
It's cold here.

Homeless, I tremble looking
at our two bodies
warm and quiet.

YOU SLEEP

Falling asleep
you ask me whether I am happy.

Over our bed, death
stands and looks at me
through your body as if through glass
with the marbles of his lidless eyes.

Under our bed
a precipice up to the stars.
Shelter my eyes with your hands
o my warm man,
shelter my eyes with your living hands.

You sleep already.

MALE AND FEMALE

You inseminated me and I gave birth to pearls.
Authentic pearls. Look.

You look, amazed,
that wealth terrifies you,
you don't understand it.

You, pebble who moved an avalanche,
look how resplendent
is its panting glamor.
Listen to a heavy hymn
of falling.

You, a pebble without eyes and ears.

ASTONISHMENT

I have been looking at you
for so many years
that you have become perfectly invisible.
But I did not realize it yet.

Yesterday
by chance I exchanged kisses with someone else.
And only then
I learned with astonishment
that for a long time
you have not been for me a man.

HE IS GONE

The finger of death touched me,
the world tumbled down
on me.

I am lying under the rubble,
hands broken,
legs broken,
backbone mangled.

People are passing
at a distance.
I call. They do not hear,
They have passed. I am dying.

The dearest man arrives.
He looks for a moment. Does not understand anything.
Leaves.

He is tenderhearted,
he is gone to comfort others.

PARTING

Our love has been dying for years.
And now our parting
suddenly resurrects it.
Our love rises from the dead
uncanny
as a corpse which came to life in order to die
for the second time.

Every night we make love,
every hour we are parting,
every hour
we swear to each other faith till the grave.

We suffer intensively,
as one suffers in hell.
Each of us runs
a 110 fever.

Moaning out of hatred
we pluck our wedding photograph from the album.
And every night till dawn,
crying, making love,
breaking into cold sweat,
we talk to each other,
we talk to each other,
we talk to each other,
for the first and the last time in life.

TEARS STREAM

They are dying, clasped tenderly to one another,
bound by their suffering
as once they were by love.
Unable to live together,
necessary to each other at that moment of dying,
close to each other
in that moment only.

Their embrace is ice,
they depart together fulfilling their oath
that they would not forsake each other till death.

Her tears
roll down his naked arm,
his tears stream
between her naked breasts.

Then
they both harden
like a sculpture on an Etruscan sarcophagus.

INTENSITY OF ATMOSPHERE

Today is my marriage
with the devil.
I go down to the bottom of the world,
brimstone and tar, the intensity of that atmosphere
chokes and enchants me.

Here is a low cave,
bedding of squalid hide.
Every place on my body once touched by your lips
will be touched now by the lips
of the monster.

They scorch me, I scream.
Their fiery touch
cauterizes my past.

Virginal in the embrace of the devil
I laugh softly.

OVER

I want to leave your hand,
your two eyes which look at me in the mirror.
Your right leg,
Your left leg,
and the rest.

Categorically I demand
to be elsewhere.
Ecstatically I demand
to be in a different manner.
I want to make myself over,
myself to make myself over.

I don't have to live,
but I myself must make myself
over.

OPEN THE DOOR OF
THE DREAM

Come to me
in a dream.
Dead, come to the dead
for the last night of love
of two beings who are no more.

It does not matter that I hate you.
It does not matter that you hate me.
That someone else is with me.
Outwit the alertness
of your thoughts which are hostile.
Outwit the alertness
of my heart which does not love you anymore.
Open softly
the door of the dream.
Dead, come to the dead.

In my dream
what has happened had not happened yet.
Thus you will kiss me
with the lips of your young happiness
and I will say to you words
more tender than I used to say in life.

It does not matter that you hate me,
it does not matter that I hate you.
Dead, come to the dead.

FIREPROOF SMILE

I found strength in myself,
no one will take it from me.
Anyone
can be replaced.
I paid for that lesson
a price it deserves.

I passed through the bath of fire,
how exquisitely
fire braces.
I carried out of it
a fireproof smile.
I won't ask anyone again
to put his hand on my head.
I will lean on
myself.

I am closed like a medieval city,
a drawbridge has been raised.
You can kill that city
but no one will enter it.

MY BODY EFFERVESCES

I am born for the second time.
I am light
as the eyelash of the wind.
I froth, I am froth.

I walk dancing,
if I wish I will soar.
The condensed lightness
of my body
condenses most forcibly
in the lightness of my foot
and its five toes.
The foot skims the earth
which gives way like compressed air.
An elastic duo
of the earth and of the foot. A dance
of liberation.

I am born for the second time,
happiness of the world
came to me again.
My body effervesces,
I think with my body which effervesces.

If I want
I will soar.

Antonia's Love
(Pages 45–65)

A BITCH

You come to me at night,
you are an animal.
A woman and an animal can be joined
by the night only.
Maybe you are a wild he-goat,
or perhaps a rabid dog.
Hard to tell in the dark.

I say tender words to you,
you don't understand, you are an animal.
You are not surprised
that sometimes I cry.

But your animal body
understands more than you do.
It, too, is sad.
And when you fall asleep
it warms me up with its hairy warmth.
We sleep hugging each other
like two puppies who lost their bitch.

A VERY SAD CONVERSATION
AT NIGHT

"You should have many lovers."
"I know, dear."
"I had many women."
"I had men, dear."
"I am finished."
"Yes, dear."
"Don't trust me."
"I don't trust you, dear."
"I am afraid of death."
"Me too, dear."
"You won't leave me."
"No, dear."
"I am alone."
"So am I, dear."
"Hug me."
"Good night, dear."

AS THE TONGUE OF
A WILD CAT

Our love is rough
as the tongue of a wild cat.

We make love
in a hammock of fire,
in sunny entrails
of the sun.

We make love
like two predatory birds
in the nest of an electric
moment.

We make love
in silence.

THE DOOR IS OPEN

No, I don't want to tame you,
you would lose your animal charm.
I am moved
by your cunning and fear,
the traits proper to your exotic race.
You won't go away,
for the door is always open,
you won't betray me,
for I do not demand faithfulness.

Give me your hand,
we will walk dancing
through darkness which is laughing.
Hieratical little bells
on our legs and hands,
a gesture of dance,
lithe as a design of the old Arabic alphabet,
a song of hair,
classically panting.

The force of rapture
organized into a mystery.
Domesticated somewhat
like you.

LOVE SEPARATES THE LOVERS

You are jealous
of the rapture which you give me,
for I betray you
with that rapture.
You give it to me as a vein of a spring
and it explodes inside me
into a river.

The river carries me
where you reach no more,
toward the paradises
you will never experience,
never understand.

We sing our love songs
in different languages,
we are strangers, enemies.
Your body is only a tool of rapture
for my body
which is so much more
noble.

I will not drown in you.
I want you to drown in me.
My laughing egoism
is my weapon and an adornment of my nakedness,
my lifebelt.

——

Skin separates the two beating hearts,
love separates the lovers.
A beautiful song of the night,
a song of combat.

A SPRING

The greatest happiness you give me
is that I don't love you.
Freedom.

I bask by you
in the warmth of that freedom,
I am meek
with the meekness of strength
and sensitive,
alert as a spring.

In all my hugs
there is a readiness to leave.
As in the body of an athlete
a future leap.

I CANNOT

I envy you. Every moment
You can leave me.

I cannot
leave myself.

IRON CURRYCOMB

Don't come to me today.
Had I half-opened the door
you wouldn't have recognized my face.
For I am busy with stocktaking,
with a capital repair, balance of accounts.
This is my washing day,
a dress rehearsal for the end of the world
in microcosm.

With an iron currycomb
I scrub my body to the bone,
I have taken the skin off the bones,
it is hanging over there,
naked intestines smoke,
naked ribs quiver
and the trial goes on,
the most high court of justice
is going to proceed in a summary manner.
All verdicts will be sentences.

It judges the brain and the eyes taken out of the skull,
the sinful nakedness of the pelvis
and of the teeth without gums,
unclean lungs, lazy tibia.
Oh, I toil hard,
with an iron currycomb
I scrub my body to the bone,
the bone to the marrow.
I want to be cleaner than the bone.

I want to be clean
as nothingness.

I judge, I carry out sentences,
I shiver with terror,
both the condemned one and the tired executioner,
I balance accounts, I sweat
with bloody sweat.

So don't come to me today.
Don't buy flowers, it's a waste of money.

GO TO A WESTERN

I enjoy equally
my greeting you and my saying good-bye.
Thus you give me
two pleasures.

But today don't come.
I have guests. A visit of
Weariness with Love's Ritual,
A Mocking Glance of Eternity and
Disgust.

They are strangers, you don't know their language.
So better go to a Western.

THE SAME INSIDE

Walking to your place for a love feast
I saw at a street corner
an old beggar woman.

I took her hand,
kissed her delicate cheek,
we talked, she was
the same inside as I am,
from the same kind,
I sensed this instantly
as a dog knows by scent
another dog.

I gave her money,
I could not part from her.
After all, one needs
someone who is close.

And then I no longer knew
why I was walking to your place.

LARGE INTESTINE

Look in the mirror. Let us both look.
Here is my naked body.
Apparently you like it,
I have no reason to.
Who bound us, me and my body?
Why must I die
together with it?
I have the right to know where the borderline
between us is drawn.
Where am I, I, I myself.

Belly, am I in the belly? In the intestines?
In the hollow of the sex? In a toe?
Apparently in the brain. I do not see it.
Take my brain out of my skull. I have the right
to see myself. Don't laugh.
That's macabre, you say.

It's not me who made
my body.
I wear the used rags of my family,
an alien brain, fruit of chance, hair
after my grandmother, the nose
glued together from a few dead noses.
What do I have in common with all that?
What do I have in common with you, who like
my knee, what is my knee to me?

———

Surely
I would have chosen a different model.

I will leave both of you here,
my knee and you.
Don't make a wry face, I will leave you all my body
to play with.
And I will go.
There is no place for me here,
in this blind darkness waiting for
corruption.
I will run out, I will race
away from myself.
I will look for myself
running
like crazy
till my last breath.

One must hurry
before death comes. For by then
like a dog jerked by its chain
I will have to return
into this stridently suffering body.
To go through the last
most strident ceremony of the body.

Defeated by the body,
slowly annihilated because of the body

———

I will become kidney failure
or the gangrene of the large intestine.
And I will expire in shame.

And the universe will expire with me,
reduced as it is
to a kidney failure
and the gangrene of the large intestine.

YOU WILL NOT REACH

In our womanly despair
so much shame.
In our looseness
so much birdsong.

Your suffering
is as shameless as your body.
You scream
with an infant's frankness. Then
I feel scorn for you.

All of you, unequivocal and heavy,
how could you understand
us, whose bodies are light
like a burst of laughter.
You don't know
the elastic bravery of a flame
which every moment destroys itself
to renew itself.
It is in us that its resilient plenty dwells,
its riches.

With you
I am other than I was with others,
from my nostril to my heel.
And a new otherness
waits in me already.
But you, when leaving me, will take

a record with only one tune
pitifully worn down.

My amorous heaven
and amorous hell
blossom high up. You will not reach them
even if only to tear them down.

I'LL OPEN THE WINDOW

Our embrace lasted too long.
We loved right down to the bone.
I hear the bones grind, I see
our two skeletons.

Now I am waiting
till you leave, till
the clatter of your shoes
is heard no more. Now, silence.

Tonight I am going to sleep alone
on the bedclothes of purity.
Aloneness
is the first hygienic measure.
Aloneness
will enlarge the walls of the room,
I will open the window
and the large, frosty air will enter,
healthy as tragedy.
Human thoughts will enter
and human concerns,
misfortune of others, saintliness of others.
They will converse softly and sternly.

Do not come anymore.
I am an animal
very rarely.

IN RAILWAY STATIONS

There, crazy hags
who carry in a bundle on their back
all their belongings.

Hobos who huddle
at night in railway stations.
Patients who wait in a hospital
for the last operation.

And I lost so much time
with you.

NONEXISTENT

Where are you, friend,
pure as plant life,
more faithful
than my own body.
The earth gives birth to millions of people
but you are not born.

There is not even a silence
waiting for your voice,
no space
waiting for the shadow
of your moving hand.

Nonexistent,
come to me.

CATCH-AS-CATCH-CAN

I catch at various things,
snow, trees, unnecessary telephones,
tenderness of a child, departures,
Różewicz's poems,
sleep, apples, morning calisthenics,
conversations on blessed effects of vitamins,
exhibits of vanguard art,
walks to Kościuszko's mound, politics,
music of Penderecki,
elemental catastrophes in distant lands,
bliss of morality and bliss of immorality,
gossip, cold shower, foreign fashion magazines,
lessons in Italian,
sympathy for dogs, the calendar.

I catch at everything
not to sink
in the abyss.

Stephanie's Love
(Pages 66–88)

A GENTLE WORLD

We are joined together by the heaven
of Fra Angelico.
His childish angels
give us their fingers.

His smile we will take in our knapsack
wandering together
through a spring world
which is gentle as the death of a blessed man.

THE YOUNGEST CHILDREN
OF AN ANGEL

When you kissed me for the first time
we became a couple
of the youngest children of an angel,
which just started
to fledge.

Lapsed into a silence in mid-move,
hushed in mid-breath,
astounded
to the very blood,
they listen with their bodies
to the sprouting on their shoulder blades
of the first little plume.

IN A CRIMSON GONDOLA

I don't love you but the happiness
which I give you.

It joins us
as a crimson gondola
joins a young doge and his bride
the day of their wedding.

VISCERA FLICKER

You gave me rapture,
I gave you rapture.
Immaculate both
we stare at each other.

In my body and in your body
pure sex
glows like amber.
Under the skin
viscera pulse with light.

You gave me purity,
I gave you purity.
The greatest purity
in the world.

DITHYRAMB OF A
HAPPY WOMAN

Song of excess,
strength, mighty tenderness,
pliant ecstasy.
Magnificence
lovingly dancing.

I quiver as a body in rapture,
I quiver as a wing,
I am an explosion,
I overstep myself,
I am a fountain,
I have its resilience.
Excess,
a thousand excesses,
strength,
song of gushing strength.

There are gifts in me,
flowerings of abundance,
curls of light are sobbing,
a flame is foaming, its lofty ripeness
is ripening.
Oceans of glare,
rosy as the palate
of a big mouth in ecstasy.

I am astonished
up to my nostrils, I snort,

a snorting universe of astonishment
inundates me.
I am gulping excess, I am choking with fullness,
I am impossible as reality.

THE FIRST MADRIGAL

That night of love was pure
as an antique musical instrument
and the air around it.

Rich
as a ceremony of coronation.
It was fleshy as a belly of a woman in labor
and spiritual
as a number.

It was only a moment of life
and it wanted to be a conclusion drawn from life.
By dying
it wanted to comprehend the principle of the world.

That night of love
had ambitions.

THE SECOND MADRIGAL

A night of love
exquisite as a
concert from old Venice
played on exquisite instruments.
Healthy as a
buttock of a little angel.
Wise as an
anthill.
Garish as air
blown into a trumpet.
Abundant as the reign
of a royal Negro couple
seated on two thrones
cast in gold.

A night of love with you,
a big baroque battle
and two victories.

AN IRON HEDGEHOG

A happy woman,
I am as an embryo in the mother's womb,
I sleep hidden in you.

Don't give birth to me yet,
I want to be in you always.
Here is my warmth,
my refuge.

Now I don't exist at all outside of you,
I am nowhere else
and that is good.

The world is freezing, I am afraid,
it is like a hedgehog with quills of iron and ice.
Do not ever give birth to me.
I want to sleep in you.

FROM THE DEPTHS OF
THE OCEAN

I am priceless as long as you are with me.
I bathe in the tub of your enchantment,
your enchantment
created me.

I give you happiness,
I can give you pain.
You offered me that power,
I bloom, you made me a queen.
My blooming enchants you,
my blooming gives joy
to you and me.

I can give you pain, you are afraid,
you are defenseless, I feel your fear.
Your fear woke up my cruelty,
I look at it, astonished
as at a beast from the depths of the ocean.

We both wonder
at its electric resilience,
your fear woos it,
they play together like young cats,
wooing each other they grow pretty.
How pretty they are now,
my cruelty and your defenselessness.

That's a fascinating game, my love.
We will stop it.

I SWEAT AND PUFF UP

You cultivate me as your own fixation
and as a rare cactus.
You attend to it
with admirable fervor.
You are a trainer.
You kneel before me,
this is the way to train
someone for sainthood.

I am supposed also to become a seraph
with six wings
and to give you a mystical happiness
as the cows give milk.

I try as I can,
I sweat and puff up,
my eyes start out of my head
from effort.

I walk obediently
in the dog collar of your adoration.

WHEN WE WAKE UP
IN THE MORNING

How good that it was,
how good that it is no more.
Thank you, dear,
for those two kinds of happiness.

Now
I have a light body and a clean soul.
My lust chemically cleansed
I violently desire,
as an asthmatic desires air,
a heavy toil,
hard human work.

My head and my hands want to work,
I am created for work,
not for bliss.
I am strong, I can carry
burdens which are carried by the strong.

BLACK POPPY

We grieve,
dread took a seat beside us.
Sadness blows into our hearts
its black poppies.
I cry,
you hug me to console me,
out of the embrace sweetness is born,
out of sweetness, a flame.

We look into each other's eyes
now brightened by our happiness.
Our bodies have given us consolation.

I AM PANTING

Why talk
if one can shout
why walk
if one can run
why live
if one can burn.

I am running and screaming with joy
I am running and screaming with despair
I am panting
my lungs work like crazy.

Violent feelings
are good, so I have heard, for your health.

KILL ME

Don't kiss me, my love.
Don't hug me, my love.
If you love me
kill me, my love.

I MUST DO IT

My very, very dear, I must part with you.
I must go away
and again I will be alone.
I will take away my body, entangled with yours
in the embrace of sleepy happiness.

It won't be easy. They two grew into one
and will defend themselves
against that rift,
as do two animals faced with death.
Terrified, stupid and beautiful
they will struggle as if for life
to keep their privilege
of night.

I must reject you, my love,
though you need me,
and go where nobody
needs me.
I must shoot you in the heart
though you beg me for mercy
and shoot myself in the heart
though I am so afraid.

No human asks me for it.
And yet I must do it.

HEAD DOWN

I kiss you and cry.
You kiss my tears and my lips
in love with my lips
and my tears

Hugging each other, unmoving
we listen to our tears falling
drop by drop
into our one heart.

I founder
into heartbreaking happiness
of love's despair,
caught in a waterfall
of bliss and suffering.
I plummet head down,
foamy water, foamy hair,
leaves, the roar of waves,
I fall,
where will I crash, on what rock,
where will I be smashed
against what bottom.

With my falling down I measure
the immensity of the world,
how splendid the world is
if one is able to suffer so.
With my misfortune I measure
the happiness of the world,

how lovely must be happiness
if misfortune is so beautiful.
Only by falling
from the summit into the abyss
can one know the summit and the abyss,
I learn
that startling knowledge.

You kiss my tears
and my lips.
You tremble, we both tremble,
we are pierced
by bliss, the suffering of love.

WE ARE GOING TO SHOOT AT THE HEART

We will kill our love.

We will strangle it
as one strangles a baby.
We will kick it
as one kicks a faithful dog.
We will tear out
its live wings
as one does it
to a bird.

We will shoot it in the heart
as one shoots
oneself.

THEY GROW INTO ONE

We must watch our bodies.
Torn apart
they grow into one in our dreams.
We must keep an eye
on the sleep of our bodies,
to pluck out of them
their dreams
as in the Middle Ages eyes were plucked out
of condemned men.

Or perhaps we will kill our bodies?
The law of life
allows us to kill our foes.

A PLATE OF SUFFERING

This morning
a vast new world
is created for me,
especially for me, what a luxury!
The world of suffering.

Outside the window a city
of the world of suffering.
Here is an authentic
street of that city.
Here is a table, a plate, a spoon.
A spoon solidly suffering, a true
plate of suffering. I will eat my breakfast
on it today.

Before my house a car and a driver
both spick-and-span,
just as if real, but this is an appearance.
Yesterday they did not exist.
They were made today
especially for me. What a luxury.

No effort was spared. Even a fly
which sits at the edge of a piece of paper
while I write, is a new one,
a fly of the world of suffering.

That world was offered to me
so suddenly.

It is a precious and rare gift
like a noose of diamonds.

I wonder at it. My hands
grow cold out of wonder.
Convex eyelids
close softly
on my eyes.

VIRGINITY

One must be brave to live through
a day. What remains
is nothing but the pleasure of longing—very precious.

Longing
purifies as does flying, strengthens as does an effort,
it fashions the soul
as work
fashions the belly.

It is like an athlete, like a runner
who will never
stop running. And this
gives him endurance.

Longing
is nourishing for the strong.
It is like a window
on a high tower, through which
blows the wind of strength.

Longing,
Virginity of happiness.

HAPPY AS A DOG'S TAIL

HAPPY AS A DOG'S TAIL

Happy as something unimportant
and free as a thing unimportant.
As something no one prizes
and which does not prize itself.
As something mocked by all
and which mocks at their mockery.
As laughter without serious reason.
As a yell able to outyell itself.
Happy as no matter what,
as any no matter what.

Happy
as a dog's tail.

I HAVE TEN LEGS

When I run
I laugh with my legs.

When I run
I swallow the world with my legs.

When I run
I have ten legs.
All my legs
shout.

I exist
only when running.

I STARVE MY BELLY FOR
A SUBLIME PURPOSE

Three days
I starve my belly
so that it learns
to eat the sun.

I say to it: Belly,
I am ashamed of you. You must
spiritualize yourself. You must
eat the sun.

The belly keeps silent
for three days. It's not easy
to waken in it higher aspirations.

Yet I hope for the best.
This morning, tanning myself on the beach,
I noticed that, little by little,
it begins to shine.

I KNOCKED MY HEAD
AGAINST THE WALL

As a child
I put my finger in the fire
to become
a saint.

As a teenager
every day I would knock my head against the wall.

As a young girl
I went out through a window of a garret
to the roof
in order to jump.

As a woman
I had lice all over my body.
They cracked when I was ironing my sweater.

I waited sixty minutes
to be executed.
I was hungry for six years.

Then I bore a child,
they were carving me
without putting me to sleep.

Then a thunderbolt killed me
three times and I had to rise from the dead three times
without anyone's help.

Now I am resting
after three resurrections.

I SLEEP AND SNORE

My legs snore,
my hands snore,
my belly snores
like insolence.
I am the capital of the empire of snoring.

The complete happiness,
so to speak.

DUEL WITH A GOD

He came to her,
a young, strong-necked god.
"I want to make love with you."
"I do, too."

He glanced and with his eyes
killed a little bird in flight.
"I am of fire,"
he said.

"I will bathe in your fire
and will transform it.
You won't kill any more
little birds."

"I am beautiful."
"I will eat your beauty
and will be rich
like the sun."

"My love kills,
the same as my sight."
"I have been killed already.
I am immortal."

He laughed,
she laughed too.
"We are going to make love,"
she said.

LONELINESS OF TALL PEOPLE

Loneliness strong
as an athlete, a strong
suffering.

The icy breath swells the lungs
to bursting, in the belly
frost burns.

Icy
needles of pathos puncture
the body to the bone, in the heart
a fettered power
beats its wings.

The fingers of the apocalypse
pull them by the hair
to heaven.
To the highest summit
of the abyss.

WE ARE GOING TO THROTTLE
EACH OTHER

I am going to walk, walk
in the greenwoods, up the mountains
till there drains out of me through my heels
my agony.

I am going to sing, sing
with my whole belly
till there spurts through my throat from my guts
my agony.

I am going to make love, love
with animals
till out of my disgust I throw up
my agony.

We are going to throttle each other
me and my bloody fate
till one of us
drops dead.

Afterword: A Dialogue

NATHAN: The voice of these poems is that of a woman seemingly isolated from or indifferent to moral and social concerns. Anna Swir's voice comes out of a place with no local reality, a time with no differentiation except moments of intensity. How does one position her in Polish poetic tradition? What would the Polish reader bring to the poems to make them seem less agonizingly pure intensity? Or is this original with her?

MILOSZ: I guess there has been a tendency in Polish poetry of the last decades to search for expression in as few words as possible. That's part, I should say, of a certain trend connected with the abandonment of meters and rhymes, which occurred in good measure before the Second World War. In Swir's case, there is a conscious attempt to practice the art of the miniature, to create a situation with a few movements of the pen. One is reminded of drawings where everything is reduced to the bodies of two lovers, and the background is hardly cast. There is a double movement: this tendency in postwar Polish poetry, and also her personal search for concision, which was already noticeable in her prewar poems.

NATHAN: In one of the poems we didn't use for this

99

anthology, a woman talks about her life. She writes:

> Wind drives me on the roads,
> wind, a deity of change,
> with puffing cheeks.
> I love that wind,
> I rejoice
> in changes.

The poem goes on to praise her solitary walks. Whether we see the wind as some *élan vital* or as the passions that drive her, there's no beginning, there's no end; all we have is what she calls "longing and the death of longing / which is called fulfillment." This is a desolate vision. More than a matter of reducing technique to some minimum, her poetry seems the expression of a strong attitude toward the nature of things. What, beyond technical interest or striving, is in this kind of poem?

MILOSZ: Perhaps, Leonard, we talk of her slightly differently now because we have received word that she died. But quite independently of that, Swir's poetry is poignant and pathetic; she exemplifies the situation of a modern woman, to a large extent. This is an emancipated woman, and, in fact, rather lonely. In the poem you quoted, she appears as moving forward, marching with the wind, drawn by the wind or pushed by that wind, and she meets companions, but basically she is alone. I feel that she presents one aspect, maybe a dim aspect, maybe a less joyous aspect, of a woman's life in the twentieth century.

NATHAN: That I can see; the poems could be taken as feminist poems.

100

Swir has a companion, Czeslaw, and that's her body. The mind and body are split, and she frequently addresses her body as if it were an animal or a stranger she happens to know well; its address to her is pain and pleasure. Often there's no way of bringing them together. You get the impression she's a materialist, but how can a materialist be a dualist? And what a lonely dualism! Her isolation is even greater than just not having a companion for very long on the road; she's not even, as it were, with her own body completely.

MILOSZ: That's a very good point that you have formulated very well: she has a companion, her body. Of course, Swir's philosophy is purely materialistic. She is outside any religion, any religious belief; she has only her body. But what I kept thinking as I read and translated her poems is that the duality of the soul and body is so persistent, something probably more fundamental than any religious belief. She reaches that gut feeling we have that we are not completely either the soul or the body. The body interferes with our soul; the soul interferes with our body.

NATHAN: And the marriage of the two is not a happy one. In the medieval debate between body and soul, the soul always gets the upper hand because it can look to a reward in heaven. One of the painful things about the debate here is that the body doesn't win, but the soul doesn't win either; they both meet the same fate.

MILOSZ: Here the soul (and be cautious now), consciousness, is confronted with the body. The body is the source of pleasure, of ecstasy—of sexual ecstasy, first of

101

all. At the same time it is an enormous burden: the body goes toward death and drags the soul together with it. Consciousness kicks against it, doesn't want to go, but is dragged by the body; and this is the whole tragedy. If we look from that point of view, we see in these passionate poems a very dramatic touch.

NATHAN: Would that, do you think, explain the anger and scorn that Swir sometimes has for her lovers? Is the real anger over the mortality of relationships, human relationships, which are the only ones that the body or the mind can look forward to—temporary relationships, transient, full of pain? Is the anger that of the mind in relation to all bodies, including those of her lovers?

MILOSZ: I guess so, because the encounter is on the level of the flesh, and there are several poems where any deeper relationship is questioned.

I would define Swir's poetry as somatic poetry. That's why I was interested in it. It is somatic poetry, but it becomes metaphysical, so to say, against her will: by faithfully describing soma, the flesh, she comes to a duality and to a nearly Platonic hatred of the flesh. It's a tremendous paradox, but she, I believe, is lucid, very brutal and lucid; you can see that.

NATHAN: Which raises another question about the technique of the poems. They're very terse; there's no involved syntax, no complicated diction. There's not much interest in psychology, certainly not of the other person; she does a very quick job of psychology in the erotic situation, but not much more. I was wondering whether

upon her experience of painting, of medieval poetry, and so on. In 1942 in Nazi-occupied Warsaw I published her long poem entitled "The Year of 1941," which was a violent and pathetic, patriotic declaration of her belief in victory over the Nazis. She had many dramatic experiences during the war, and after the war she started to look for means of expressing those experiences. She gradually found a form somewhat similar to her earlier miniatures, but now much more realistic, relating not to painting and to old poetry, but to snapshots. (When reading those poems I sometimes thought about poets of the very beginning of our century, such as the French poet Blaise Cendrars, who published a volume of documentaries originally called *Kodak*.) She made two attempts, I should say. Soon after the war she published a number of such prose poems, snapshots of situations. And then many years later, some thirty years later, she succeeded in writing a cycle of short poems on her experiences as a military nurse in the Warsaw Uprising of 1944, which were published as a volume, *Building the Barricade*. Her poems can be divided into those where she speaks as a persona, speaks about her direct experience, and those which are objective, those which describe things she knows actually happened but where her persona doesn't appear. I guess the reader who has read only poems in our selection would have difficulty in guessing another side of Anna Swir's personality. So it seems appropriate here to read a few of the war poems, first from her initial attempt and then from those poems about the Warsaw Uprising. Here is a quite objective poem, "A Truck," which very naturalistically describes how people were executed in Warsaw and other Polish cities. (The image of that period, popular in the U.S., that horrors were perpetrated only against the Jews, is not quite correct. Gentile hostages, so-called hostages, were often taken and executed.) "A Truck" is a prose poem.

That street is often busy at night. Bouncing on cobblestones a truck passes, carrying people who stand in a ringing frost, with bare heads and in paper suits. Their hands are bound behind their backs by barbed wire. Their mouths are sealed with plaster.

The escorting soldier with a glimmer of a cig-arette in his lips, his rifle at the ready, sweeps gloomily with his eyes the dumb windows and gates of the lifeless city.

He is somewhat sleepy after yesterday's bout of drinking and probably for that reason he does not notice that on a first floor a windowpane flick-ered in the light of the moon. Someone noiselessly half-opens a window and, standing, makes a sign with his hand to those who ride to their death.

One of them sees him.

So that's an objective situation. Another poem, "A Manhunt," is about the Gestapo, who would come any time, day or night, and arrest people.

It was late afternoon. Lights were already lit here and there in the town and a powdery snow-storm began to blow in earnest through deserted streets, when somebody put his hand silently on the door handle.

It did not appear ominous at all and the man
who stepped up to the door holding a sleepy child
on his shoulder did not know that the house was
surrounded.

Or there are poems about the ghetto, scenes from its final
destruction after the ghetto uprising, when whole streets
were burned, one after another.

Ghetto: Two Living Children

Screaming ceased long ago on that street. Only
the wind sometimes plays with a torn-out window
in which the remnants of a windowpane still glit-
ter, and carries over the cobblestones feathers from
ripped-open eiderdowns.

The same wind brings at times from far off a
sudden shout of many people. Then it happens
that from a cross street unexpectedly two living
children walk out. Holding each other's hands they
escape silently through the middle of a deserted
street.

Up to the spot where, hidden behind a street
corner wrapped in mist, a German soldier at a
machine gun watches day and night on the border
of the ghetto.

And here is a poem that is more personal, "A Hospital
Blanket," which we may consider a passage to her cycle
of poems from the Warsaw Uprising. Swir speaks of her
situation as a military nurse.

Under that same hospital blanket with which
I cover myself after a sleepless night, four men

had died this week. Four soldiers—I remember their death agony.

I pull over myself the side less stained with blood and fall asleep on the corridor floor, by a civilian who gasped and rattled there for twenty-four hours, and just now stopped and stiffened. They cover him already.

I fall asleep for a short while, as the sky outside the window whitens already and the first morning bird has already sung in the cold. In a moment a nurse will tug at the sleeve of my uniform.

"Five o'clock, time to take the patients' temperature."

And now two personal poems from the Warsaw Uprising.

When a Soldier Is Dying

By the stretcher, on the floor
I knelt close to him,
I kissed his tunic,
I was saying: you are beautiful,
you can give so much happiness,
you don't know yourself how much happiness,
you will live, my beautiful,
my brave boy.

He smiled and he listened,
his eyelids heavier and heavier,
he did not know that such words
are said to a soldier
only when he is dying.

A Conversation Through the Door

At five in the morning
I knock on his door.
I say through the door:
In the hospital at Sliska Street
your son, a soldier, is dying.

He half-opens the door,
does not remove the chain.
Behind him his wife
shakes.

I say: your son asks his mother
to come.
He says: the mother won't come.
Behind him the wife
shakes.

I say: the doctor allowed us
to give him wine.
He says: please wait.

He hands me a bottle through the door,
locks the door,
locks it with a second key.

Behind the door his wife
begins to scream as if she were in labor.

And here is a poem, "I Am Afraid of Fire," where her persona also speaks. This is a very, very realistic picture because there were whole streets burning from the shelling. She is running through such a street. I know very few poems where the presence of fire is so powerfully felt.

I Am Afraid of Fire

Why am I so afraid
running in the street
that is burning.

After all, there are no people here
only fire buzzing up to the sky
and that crash is not a bomb,
it's only three floors collapsed.

Naked liberated flames dance,
they wave their arms
through the holes of windows.
It's sinful
to spy on
naked flames,
it's sinful to eavesdrop
on the speech of free fire.

I run away from that speech
which resounded on the earth
earlier than the speech of man.

NATHAN: These poems prompt another question—
maybe unanswerable. A poem like "Fire" sounds very
much like Swir's erotic poems in style. Why after the war
did she so drastically reduce her subject matter almost
exclusively to erotic poetry, except for *Building the Barricade*? Did she see the "wars" of sex, of mind and body—
stripped of romance and hope—as a sort of measure for
all other experience?

MILOSZ: That's very hard to answer. However, my
impression is that even as a young girl she was of a rather

skeptical, ironic nature. Maybe her upbringing helps explain this. As she tells it, she grew up in the workshop of her father, a painter, and she would do her lessons sitting on the floor; she was surrounded with paintings by her father, reproductions of paintings, and easels. And she was very poor, extremely poor. I guess a kind of dry irony found its way into her early poems: stylized, very aesthetic miniatures about artists. That was one factor. Another, of course, was the experience of war, but I should draw your attention to one thing which to me is rather strange: she seems to have only one kind of religion, and that is patriotism. Absolute devotion to her country. Patriotism goes together strangely with her dry, ironic outlook. It's very hard to visualize a person who is not only ironic, but also sarcastic about herself and about her body, about really everything, who at the same time recognizes the true value of heroism, of the duty of soldiers. My guess is that a poet may change considerably during his or her lifetime but basic orientations are always there. Of course it may be that the war experiences marked her, but not so that she would become a completely different person.

NATHAN: I didn't make myself too clear. Maybe I can put the question this way: After an experience like the war, why would she choose—or be driven to—a subject that seems so unrelated to war and so deliberately limiting? I can see why war might push an already lean style to an even harsher leanness, but I can't see why it would push her toward a subject so different.

MILOSZ: You mean love.

NATHAN: Love.

MILOSZ: Well, it's curious that she started to write, or at least to publish, love poems when she was sixty. But these poems, like her war poems, probably had a long history of revisions. Basically, the subject of all her poetry is love and death, two elemental things. And I shouldn't say that her poetry is very rich as it stands now; I should say that it is obsessive, poignant, terse, reduced to a certain narrow range. Why? Perhaps because of the constant effort to be concise, and not to go beyond her capabilities, since if you use a dry pen and you do little drawings, you cannot be a Rembrandt. Rembrandt did little drawings too, but he also did other things.

NATHAN: If she is a miniaturist, it seems to me she is an abstract one. As you say, the situations are filled out with a few strokes, the characters are nameless, the locale anywhere. It's almost geometrical, a matter of line more than color, of form more than substance. And this concentration makes for the peculiar intensity of the poems. This I see, but where does the patriotism you were speaking of spring from? How can her ruthless irreverence about things romantic or religious be squared with her worship of her nation as almost a religious object?

MILOSZ: That's a very good question. In Polish literature there is a very strong tradition of Romantic activist poetry; after all, the struggle for independence lasted throughout the whole nineteenth century and endowed the national identity with a sacred aura. There are some poems by Swir in which she speaks of the Polish earth

111

receiving ashes, blood, everything, as though in a religious sacrifice. This devotion is something that unites Polish atheists and Polish believers. Outsiders might ask: Why are Polish churches full? Why are there pilgrimages to the shrine of the so-called Black Madonna in which both believers and nonbelievers participate? All this cannot be reduced to a purely political position against the Communist government. It is, rather, an affirmation of basic values, of the existence of good and evil, a basic attachment to meaning. So Anna Swir is very much in the current tradition. You see, these things may be somewhat difficult for foreigners; it is assumed that the liberated woman, a woman who doesn't belong to any religious denomination, should be liberated as far as her country is concerned. But that's not true in the case of the Poles.

NATHAN: Isn't it strange, though, that she has one set of poems—exclusively about war—in her closet, another set—mostly about love—on her desk, as if they had no connection? Did she think perhaps that to bring the two subjects together would be somehow to debase the war poems? Other poets—Sappho at the very beginning of our tradition and Amichai today—mix these subjects, using one to illuminate the other. It's strange to me how much she compartmentalized these two obsessive subjects, except in the poem about the dying soldier. Is this a legitimate puzzlement on my part?

MILOSZ: I'm not sure, because her war poems are not abstract but are always snapshots of a human situation: there is a human being, or a group of human beings, in every poem. And there are a lot of poems about hospitals,

112

civil hospitals after the war, about people terminally ill, about all the women in the hospitals. And there are ferociously feminist poems that are really class-war poems: the males are oppressors, the women are proletarians . . . terse poems of how women are treated by those brutes, males. So there are bridges.

NATHAN: Is there any Western writer Swir is at all comparable to?

MILOSZ: Not that I'm able to think of. As I have said already, there were European poets at the very beginning of our century with their passion for reality. Swir wants to touch reality proper; she is, I would say, naturalistic. For me it's very strange because I cannot think of any woman poet in the English language with a similar fierceness in trying to be close to reality. After all, there are many women poets who write about physical love. What do *you* think?

NATHAN: Well, I was thinking of someone like Sylvia Plath. Readers might say: ah, the connection here is this brutal honesty; but in fact we best know Plath for poems of confession, something Swir doesn't engage in; she's not a confessional poet. It might appear that way when she talks very openly about relations, but you look at the relations and, as we've said, they're almost impersonal. So no, I don't think she's really like American poets. Nor is her work like—the word is "naked," the naked poetry of a generation back. She's not giving us a glimpse of her "real" life in the sense that American poets are. No, I can't think of anyone who's quite like her.

MILOSZ: I cannot find an example in either French poetry or in Russian poetry. She stands as a very peculiar phenomenon.

NATHAN: Nothing in Polish either, no one like her?

MILOSZ: I should mention Tadeusz Różewicz, whose poetry is similar. I guess she may have been influenced by him; his poetry has been defined by a critic as a "casket-oriented somatism." And it is said of him that he was marked by his wartime experiences when he was in the Resistance, and since that time a completely desperate view of human beings as flesh that is condemned to die is a permanent feature of his poetry. So she's not alone in this respect.

NATHAN: One more question. Is it possible to divide Polish poets, those writing since or from just before the war, into two sets, a very rough classification: those that were driven by that catastrophe and its aftermath to find a reduced style to match their reduced hopes, and those that have sought a richer style to—I don't quite know, maybe to find somewhere in experience meanings lost in the war? Is this too simple a division and is it particularly Polish?

MILOSZ: No; it seems to me, Leonard, that we have here the general problem of world literature, the problem of basic existential despair, and the person who comes to my mind is Samuel Beckett. Undoubtedly poetry like that of Anna Swir or Różewicz is in some respects of that general existential mold. Of course, Swir and Różewicz went through certain war experiences, and that's an excellent bridge to reach that road. But Samuel Beckett didn't go through such things, and he took that road. I don't know, I wouldn't like to be too ponderous and overburden poor Anna Swir with too much of a philosophical load, but we have to confront the issue, namely that we live in a very peculiar historical period. Life after death was a very strong ingredient of our civilization for many centuries; images of heaven and hell were with us for millennia. The question of salvation and damnation today may be dealt with by people who are religious believers and those who are not believers, but even the believers do not have any images of paradise or hell. Perhaps people who die for Khomeini have a vision of traditional Muslim paradise, but this is a peculiar situation. And that's why body, diet, vitamins, hospitals, and medicine in general are so much the center of our attention.

NATHAN: That leaves us with this world and no other.

MILOSZ: Maybe that would be going too far. As for Anna Swir, yes, I guess so. But not for everybody. Yet Anna Swir presents a serious challenge not so much to belief as to the images of belief. Think of *The Divine Comedy* and the presence of the other world in it. Personally, I feel the dead are present and part of our lives but, being a modern poet, I am unable to put them in any imaginary space. And for poetry—now we discuss not religion but poetry, which uses images—it's very important, isn't it?

NATHAN: If poetic imagination is a true means of knowing the world and what may lie behind it, yes, terribly important. But as in other matters here, we run into a

115